ABOUT THIS BOOK

Bradford is a gerbil. He lives in secret comfort behind the closet wall of a house owned by an absent-minded old lady. In return for her unintentional hospitality, Bradford guards her money which she keeps hidden in an old shoe in her closet.

One day when Miss Tilly is away, a man in a black felt hat sneaks up the walk to her front door. Bradford's fast thinking frightens the stranger away this time, but will he return? Read and find out what a small but very smart gerbil does to protect an old lady and her money.

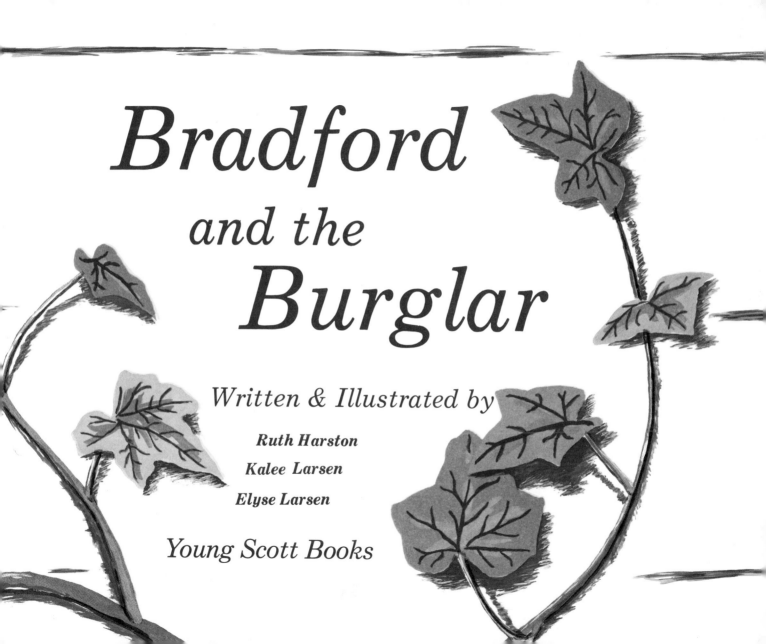

Bradford
and the
Burglar

Written & Illustrated by

Ruth Harston

Kalee Larsen

Elyse Larsen

Young Scott Books

Until just a few years ago, all gerbils (pronounced *jerbul*) lived in Asia. Now, many of them live in other places. Some live in cages and belong to boys and girls who keep them as pets.

But Bradford lives in a little room behind Miss Tilly's closet in a large old house. This is not surprising, for Bradford is different from other gerbils in many ways.

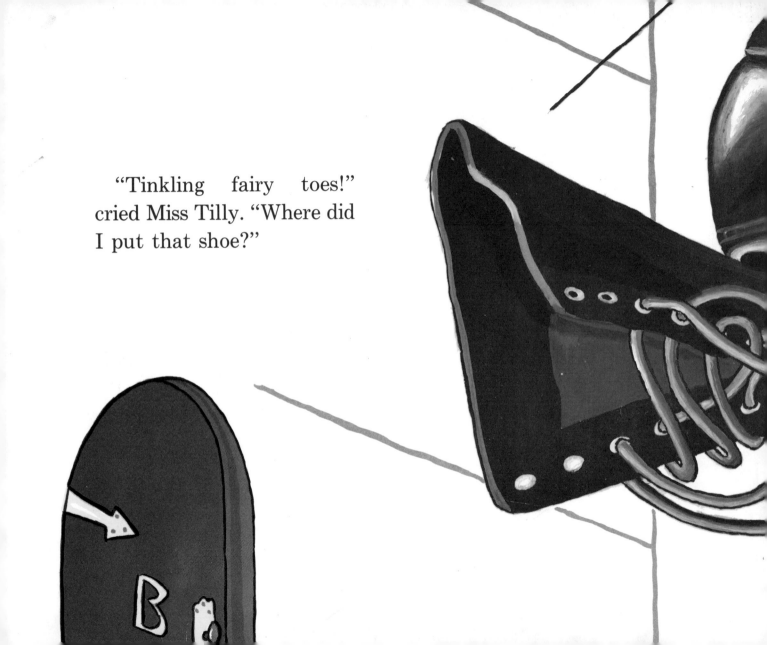

"Tinkling fairy toes!" cried Miss Tilly. "Where did I put that shoe?"

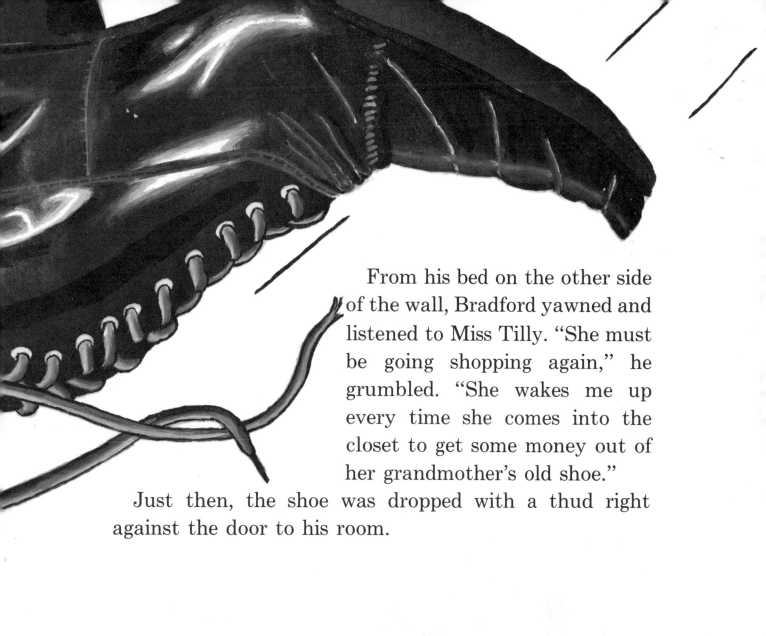

From his bed on the other side of the wall, Bradford yawned and listened to Miss Tilly. "She must be going shopping again," he grumbled. "She wakes me up every time she comes into the closet to get some money out of her grandmother's old shoe."

Just then, the shoe was dropped with a thud right against the door to his room.

Bradford pushed back his quilt and jumped out of bed. Then he went to his dresser and brushed his fur until it shone.

"Miss Tilly will be out for a while. Good! Now I'll have a chance to practice the piano," he thought.

As soon as Bradford heard the front door slam, he danced through his own front door—right into Miss Tilly's shoe! He backed out and stuffed a stray dollar bill down into the toe.

"I wish Miss Tilly would keep her money in the bank like other people," Bradford muttered crossly. "Sooner or later somebody is going to find out about the money shoe and steal it from her."

"Oh," thought Bradford after he had moved the shoe. "Now, I'd better go check to make sure Miss Tilly hid her key when she left. She's so careless!"

Bradford hurried back into his room, climbed out his window, and scurried down the ivy. He ran around to the front of the house just as a man in a black felt hat was approaching the door.

"He's no friend of Miss Tilly's," said Bradford.

Bradford looked up at the front door. "The key!" he squeaked. "It's still in the lock. Oh dear, oh dear!"

Just then Bradford spied the sprinkler by the front door. He ran over to the water faucet and turned it on with all his might.

The man jumped with surprise as water spurted into the air. He dropped the key and ran down the sidewalk.

Bradford turned off the water and went to the front door to check on the key. "Whew! That was a close call!" he panted. "I wonder if that man knows about Miss Tilly's money."

Bradford slid the key under the doormat, where Miss Tilly meant to put it, then hid in the bushes. "My practicing will have to wait. I'll stand guard until Miss Tilly gets home," he said.

Sure enough, Bradford saw the man in the black felt hat walk back up the street and look all around. Then he crouched down behind the hedge to watch the house.

Bradford was frantic. The sprinkler probably wouldn't scare the man away again. What could he do?

Then Bradford thought of his mortal enemy, Bowzer, the dog next door. Bradford hated that dog, and always tried to keep as far away from him as he could; but maybe, just maybe, Bowzer could help him now.

Bradford ran across the lawn and climbed through the fence. Bowzer was chained to the clothesline, and as long as Bradford didn't get too close, the dog couldn't reach him.

This morning, Bowzer was asleep. From a safe distance, Bradford squeaked to try to wake him, but his gerbil squeak was not nearly loud enough. Bowzer slept on.

Bradford got more and more desperate.

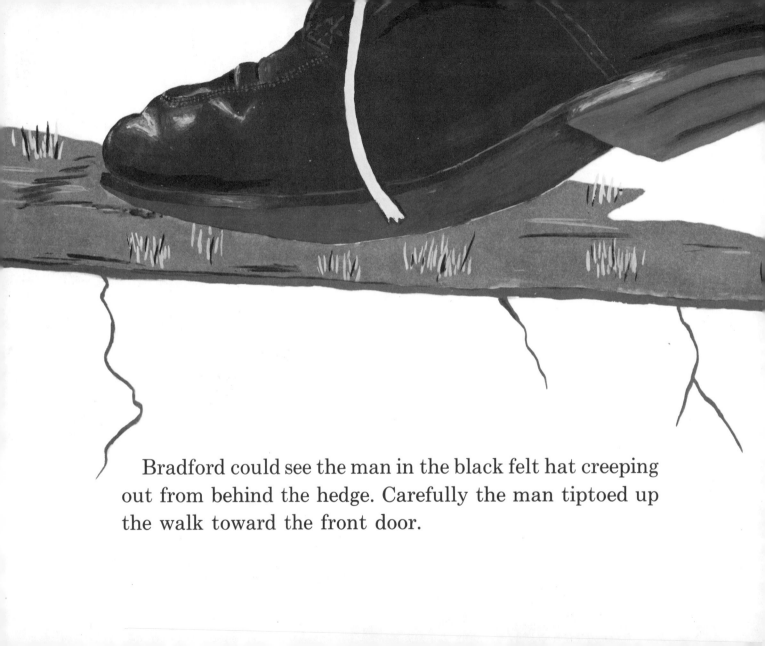

Bradford could see the man in the black felt hat creeping out from behind the hedge. Carefully the man tiptoed up the walk toward the front door.

Bradford shouted himself hoarse, but Bowzer still slept on. There was only one thing left for him to do. Afraid for his life, but knowing he had a duty to perform, he dashed up to Bowzer and bit his tail—hard!

Bowzer was up in an instant. "EEOOOOW!" he howled. Barking loudly, he strained at his leash to get at Bradford.

But Bradford was too quick for him. He ran back home as fast as he could, just in time to see the frightened burglar run down the sidewalk.

Bradford went to the front door and lifted a corner of the mat to make sure the key was still there. It was.

He sighed with relief.

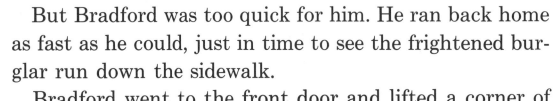

A few minutes later, Miss Tilly came up the walk carrying a bag of groceries. Bradford hid behind the bush and watched her. She reached under the doormat for the key, unlocked the door, and went inside.

Bradford groaned. Miss Tilly had forgotten to take the key out of the lock again! He climbed the screen and removed the key. He waited outside until he heard Miss Tilly playing the piano in the living room. Then he dragged the key into the house and put it on the kitchen table.

"An exhausting morning," said Bradford, "and I didn't even get a chance to practice." He went to his room, ate some sunflower seeds, then dropped on his bed to rest.

Bradford spent the afternoon trying to read, but he couldn't keep his mind on the story. He kept thinking about the man in the black felt hat. "He'll be back," he said to himself, "but when, I wonder?"

That night Bradford was a bit nervous as he prepared for bed. "Will the man come back tonight?" he worried. "I hope not. It's been a very busy day and I'm tired."

Bradford blew out the lamp on his dresser and climbed into bed. Finally he dropped off to sleep, dreaming of black felt hats.

Soon the big white house was dark and still.

Crash! Bradford awoke with a start. A big hand was reaching at him through his window. Bradford knew in an instant who it was. He sprang from his bed just as the hand withdrew. He peeked out and saw the man in the black felt hat climbing up the drainpipe on the side of the house to Miss Tilly's bedroom window.

"Oh, what shall I do?" groaned Bradford. "He's going to steal Miss Tilly's money!"

Bradford could hear the man in the black felt hat creeping into Miss Tilly's closet.

Two big hands began shoving shoe boxes aside, looking for something special. "At last!" he whispered greedily, as his hand closed around an old-fashioned shoe. The man sighed with satisfaction as he reached in for the crisp roll of bills.

But who do you think was inside the shoe waiting for that hand? Bradford! Quick as a flash, he sprang at a finger and bit it hard.

"OWWWWW!" howled the burglar.

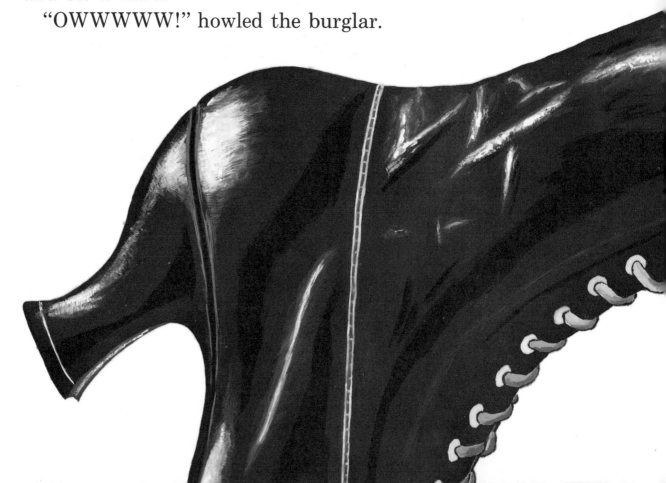

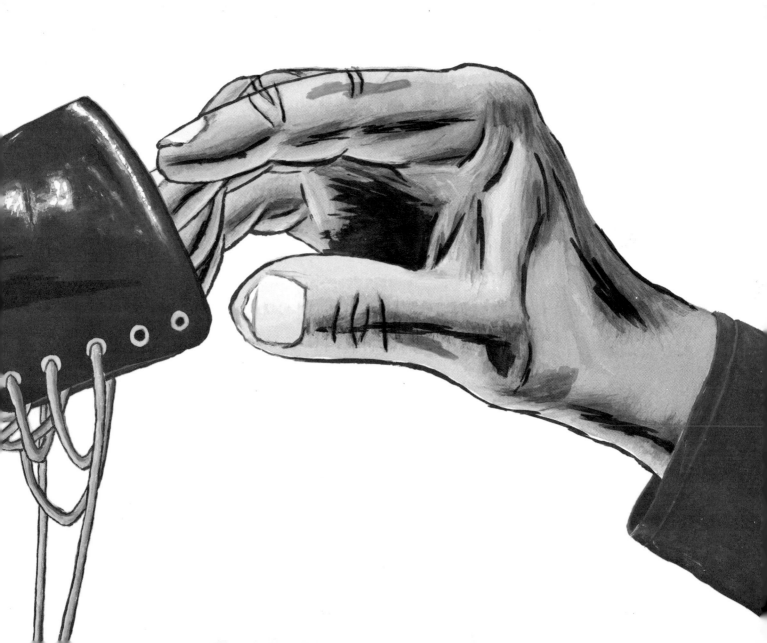

Now, Miss Tilly could sleep through an earthquake, or a thunderstorm, or a hurricane; but that howl jolted her out of bed in an instant. She saw the burglar running for the window. Screaming with all her might, she snatched her hairbrush from the dresser and lunged at the burglar.

Just before his head disappeared out the window, Miss Tilly gave him a whack. He lost his balance and plunged to the ground.

"Tinkling fairy toes!" gasped Miss Tilly. "He must be dead!"

With trembling hands, she dialed the police. Her voice shook as she told them where they could find the man.

Then she collapsed on the bed, too weak to move.

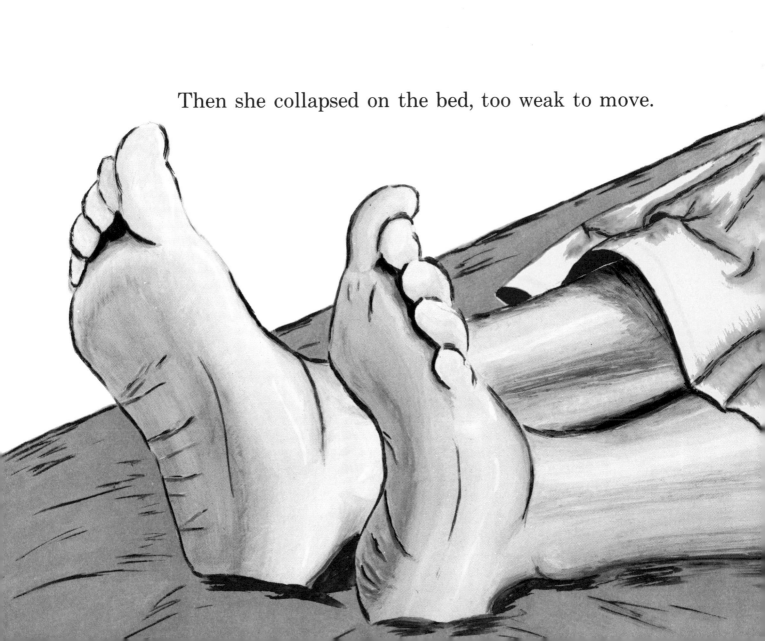

Bradford ran back to his room. He leaned out of his broken window just in time to see the burglar hit the ground. The man—with the black felt hat no longer over his eyes—moaned and slowly began to pull himself up.

Bradford was expecting this. He ran to his food basket and picked out the largest walnut he could find. Taking careful aim, he flung it at the burglar's head. This surprise attack was too much for the man. He slumped back to the ground.

As the sound of the police siren grew louder, Bradford nodded to himself with satisfaction. He had saved Miss Tilly's money, and—who knows, maybe even her life! There couldn't be a better way of paying for his room and board. Besides, a little excitement was just to his liking.